To Arlene !

MAX THE DRAGON SLAYER

Eph. 6:12

Merry S. Streeter

Merry S. Streeter

D1737050

For more information, contact :
MERRY.S.STREETER@GMAIL.COM

Cover design and art by Merry S. Streeter
ISBN: 9798702131009

Published May 2023

CONTENTS

MVFOL

*To my husband, Rick,
and our whole brood!
I love you with all my heart.*

FOREWARD

After 25 years in professional ministry as a Youth Pastor and 20 years now as a Senior Pastor, I'm pretty used to people just accepting what I say without question (or, if they DO question me, it's out of my earshot!)

And then along came Merry Streeter!

I first met Merry many years ago when I was the Youth Pastor at the church where her children attended. They were active members of our Youth Ministry. Like many parents, Merry often had questions about something I had taught her kids. Unlike many parents, Merry ALWAYS had follow-up questions and insights of her own. I soon realized that THIS mother would challenge me to really know what I'm talking about and what I believe!

Now, don't get me wrong, when I say she 'challenged' me, I don't mean that in a disrespectful way. Merry's desire has always been to know Him, grow in our knowledge of God's Word, and our relationship with each other. In the decades we've known each other (for many years now, I've been HER Pastor!) I can honestly say Merry has taught me as much, if not more than I've taught her (although…who's keeping score!) The Apostle Paul could have been speaking of Merry when he wrote I Thessalonians 5:11, *"Therefore, encourage one another, and build one another up, just as you also are doing!"*

Max The Dragon Slayer is yet another example of that encouragement. Merry's knowledge of the youth culture immediately drew me into the story. These young people

3

and their experiences ring true, and that aspect of this story is very refreshing!

But then, Merry's ability to see below the surface kicks in, and that takes the story into a whole new dimension! Yes, Sunday School teaches us that there are 'unseen forces' arrayed against us, but what does that LOOK like? Once again, Merry is challenging me...and I am so much better for it!

I would encourage parents and young people to read this story together and then discuss what you've read. Allow this to be a tool that can take your conversations, and your relationships, into areas where you may not have been before. Let it challenge you to go back to God's Word and check what's been said. I'll warn you, you probably won't agree on everything (indeed, Merry and I don't agree on everything, and that, in fact, *energizes* our conversations!), but don't be afraid of that! It's good practice for our world today, where any two people probably have three (or more!) opinions!

As she's challenged me these many years (and continues to challenge me), allow Merry to now challenge and encourage you! Trust me; you'll be much better for it!

Enjoy *Max The Dragon Slayer!*

Pastor Willie Behrends
CrossWinds Church of Moreno Valley, CA

1

ECHO AND THE DRAGON

Max froze in his tracks. He saw kids standing in a circle poking something with sticks, laughing and chattering. *What was it?* He'd been wandering in the field near his house looking for his dog.

He worried. *Was it Echo?* His Siberian Husky had been missing for over an hour. Running to the ring of kids, he squeezed his head through their shoulders to see a deer's head lying on a card table, brains exposed. A hunter left it after removing the antlers. Max watched the kids inspecting this gooey head while some brought their hands up to their mouths at the empty stare of its glazed eyes. He sighed, relieved they weren't jabbing Echo and turned to leave to search for his dog.

"Echo! Echo!" called Max, looking right and left. "*Woof, Woof!*"

Max's green eyes grew wide. He sprinted down a dirt path toward the barking!" "*Ouch!*" Max scraped his shin on an overgrown brush as he made his way.

"Oh, there you are, Echo!"

And there he was. His collar caught on a low tree branch trapping him while Max noticed a rabbit 20 yards down the dirt path watching his attacker struggle.

Echo howled and swung his fluffy tail wildly at the sight of his buddy. Max threw his arms around Echo, hugging him tightly as the dog licked Max's entire face.

When Echo finally stilled, the boy gently clipped the leash onto the dog's collar, noticing a strange toy lying across the path. Max's eyes shot back to the dog as he snapped the branch like a straw, loosening Echo from his trap. Kids didn't leave toys so far in the field.

Once freed, Max gripped the leash hard and glanced at the strange toy across the path again. Peering closer, he could see it was a dragon…a dragon toy. *Huh. That's weird*, thought Max. He'd never seen anything like this toy before. Echo lunged and his boy toward home, and the two ran through the field, jumping over mounds and gopher holes. Max forgot all about the sting of the scratches; he was happy to have Echo again!

They ran up the stairs into the house and saw his older brother, Miles, eyes sharpened against him.

"Where have you been?" Miles asked as he watched his brother walk toward his room. "Mom told you to take the trash out!"

"I went looking for Echo, Miles!" I couldn't find him at home, so I looked in the field."

"Well, you better do what Mom said right away, or I'll tell her you just left your chores to play."

Max couldn't understand why Miles wasn't glad to see him and Echo and why he often tried to get him into trouble.

Echo lapped water from his dish, his huge tongue sending puddles on the floor, but Max was relieved Echo was back home. Grabbing an old towel from the kitchen counter, he wiped the spilled water as Miles glared at him from the kitchen corner.

2

MEETING LIAM

C ome on, Echo," Max said as he tramped down the hall to his bedroom. Echo wagged his tale, following. Max flopped on his bed, tired. The dog also jumped onto the bed, licking Max's arm. "Stop!" Max said, pushing Echo away and laying back, covering himself to sleep. *Tomorrow is Monday, a school day. Ugh.*

Max yawned. Hitting him right in the eyes, a beam of light snuck through a crack in the closed curtains--he squeezed his eyelids tighter, then Mom burst in a moment later.

"Time to get up, Max! Don't be late for school!" she said.

Groggy, Max slowly opened both eyes, blinking, but Echo popped up, ready to follow Max wherever he went. Max rolled out while Echo hopped off, and both headed to the bathroom. The dog lay on the floor watching Max brush his teeth and run a comb through his unruly brown hair.

Afterward, Max rushed downstairs, grabbed a snack bar for his blue Sport backpack, and dashed out the door as the bus gave no wiggle room today. Echo watched from the living room window and barked. It came right on time—8:10 am.

The bus ride was always noisy, but Max and his friends, Logan and Mason, enjoyed being together.

"Let's play "Would You Rather," Logan said.

"Okay," Max said.

"Would you rather be a cat or an eagle?" Logan

asked Max.

"Uh...an eagle!"

"Okay, and why? Logan asked.

"Because I can fly high and see everything from the sky."

"Your turn, Max!" Logan said.

"Okay, Mason, would you rather...*Bump*! Logan shifted against Mason as the bus jolted to a stop.

"Sorry!" said Logan, and they arrived at the school. Max, Logan, Mason, and the other kids piled out of the bus.

As the stream of kids flowed into the school building from their parent's cars and buses, his best friend, Mason, wearing a red plaid shirt, chattered, carrying his trombone case. Mason bumped past the other students heading for class. Max practically tripped over Mason, his best friend, as he avoided a group of girls. Seeing the boys dart around them, Naomi, Jordan, and Hailey giggled.

"Hey Mason, Watch out! You're going to hit me with that trombone case." Max smiled and patted Mason on the back. "Trombones are dangerous. I keep telling you that." Still smiling.

Logan jogged over to Max after retying his shoe. "Hey, Max!" said Logan with a smile creasing his freckled cheeks. "You wanna go with me to church this

Sunday?"

Max tilted his head. "Church?" asked Max.

"Yeah, we're having a special day to bring our friends from school! And... they're giving everyone a prize if we do!" said Logan. He gave his friend a pop on the shoulder as they strode into class.

Max noticed Liam as he sat in the second to the last row, a few chairs down from him. He'd seen this boy keeping to himself often, and today he sat head down, hand in pocket.

Liam was a loner. He loved spell-books and tarot cards, especially wizards and witchcraft games. But as Liam sat at his desk, he took something black from his pocket, looked at it, talked to it, then put it back. The teacher droned on and on until the bell rang. It took forever for recess.

Something inside Liam wanted to be friends with Logan, Mason, and Max. They *were* friendly boys. Logan was the church kid, Mason was the music man, and Max, well, he just loved sports. When recess came, the three boys ran outside and grabbed a soccer ball to play a game. Mason tripped but caught himself. Max chuckled, stumbling as he raced. They both laughed, relieved to be outside. Logan bolted out to the field. Max liked having him come along to play with the soccer ball since he could run and kick well. From the corner of his eye, Max could see Liam sitting alone at a table, looking down, his arms around his knees. He pulled something out of his pocket again, talked to himself, and put it back. Max wondered what he was doing and called out.

"Hey Liam, wanna join us?"

Liam looked up, black hair hanging over his eyes, "Uh... okaaay."

"What?" Max asked, not hearing Liam.

"Oh...uh...sure!" Liam said louder. He sat up, jumped off the table, and walked over. Logan strolled over to him and being a good sport, patted him on the back and said, "Let's play!"

Max, Mason, and stocky Logan kicked the soccer ball back and forth to each other, running fast, but Liam couldn't keep up. He was skinny and awkward, stumbled often, and missed the ball.

"I'm not going to play anymore!" Liam said.

"Whoa, hey, wait a minute Liam," Max said, "we'll take it down a notch!"

The sun was hot, and Max saw Logan was anxious. He wanted competition but knew they took it easy trying to be a friend to Liam. So, they played more gently, kicking the ball to Liam often. Logan jumped up and down while playing, wishing the game would get harder.

"Time for a break," Max said. They stopped and

walked over to sit under a tree to rest.

"Hey, Max, have you thought about what I asked you?" Logan said.

"What was that again?"

"You know when I asked you if you would come to church with me," Logan said.

Upon hearing this, Liam bristled, scrunched his nose, then wriggled, sitting beside Max.

"You know Logan... why not?" said Max. "Sure. I'll go with you. I need to ask Mom and Dad, though."

"Great!" said Logan. "Hey, what about you, Liam? Wanna go to church with me this Sunday?"

Liam wrinkled his nose again. His black eyes rolled, then he got up and quickly walked away. Max scratched his head as Logan and Mason looked at each other. "Was it something I said?" asked Logan.

The boys sat quietly, looked at each other, and shrugged.

3

OH, ECHO!

The school bell rang. Kids flooded out of the building, and the bus waited until all were on board, then chugged away to drop each one off at their house.

Max was not happy to go home to an empty house. Mom and Dad were working. His little sister, Marian, was in daycare, and his brother, Miles, was in an after-school band program. *At least Echo was there,* thought Max. His dog was always happy to see him.

Max found the chrome key and opened the door

to find trash all over the living room!

"Oh no!" cried Max. "I forgot to take the trash out!" It was everywhere. In the living room, the kitchen, the den, the bathroom...*ugh,* sighed Max. Echo was nowhere to be seen... again!

"Where are you, Echo?" Once, his dog had chewed a pillow and left pieces strewn all over the living room. He hid whenever he did something he knew was a no-no.

Max walked around the house looking, and... there he was! A tail poked out from behind the curtain in the living room.

"Echo! What have you done?!" Echo peeked around the curtain with guilty eyes. "Come on, Echo. You're going outside!"

Max dragged the dog out into the unmowed backyard and closed the door to begin to clean up. He collected used napkins, empty cans, and crushed cereal boxes. Even coffee grounds were spread all over the kitchen floor. *Gross*, thought Max.

Echo started to bark and scratch at the back door to come in. Max peeked out the front living room window to see the family had come home. They were piling out of the car, about to trek up their long driveway. He swept fast, let Echo back in, ran to the living room, turned on the TV, and jumped onto the couch, feet up on the coffee table.

Within minutes, the door opened. Marian, Miles, Mom, and Dad walked in. Max was watching TV as if nothing had happened.

"Did you do your homework?" Mom asked. "Ummm...I...Ummm...I."

"Max, you know that's the first thing you must do when you get home!" said Mom. "Now, march to your bedroom and start working on it!"

Miles flashed an evil grin that Max had gotten into trouble. He socked Max in the arm as he walked by.

Max didn't tell his mom what happened with Echo. He'd be in trouble and didn't want that. It was already hard to take Miles' taunts. Max dragged up the stairs with Echo in tow.

Then he remembered. Logan invited him to church! *I need to go ask Mom and Dad!* he thought. He turned around and walked back downstairs. Mom was busy in the kitchen. Dad was watching TV with Marian.

"Mom, Logan asked if I would come to church this Sunday. Would that be all right?"

"Hmm. I guess so. Just be sure you get all your homework done right after school, okay?"

"Yes, Mom," Max said.

Miles had an idea.

Sunday morning came quickly. Max was excited. He'd not been to church in a long time and never to Logan's! He picked out his clothes from the messy drawers, some were wrinkled, but at least they were clean!

Then he heard, *Honk, Honk!*

Max went to get his Bible but couldn't find it. He called out, "Anyone seen my Bible?"

"Not me!" shouted Marian shaking her curly blonde head.

"Not me!" said Miles, grinning and satisfied he'd made Max late.

Max pushed his books around and opened his drawers. *Nowhere.*

Miles had hidden Max's Bible.

Honk, Honk!

"Don't make them wait!" Mom cried out.

"Get going!" Dad said.

Max ran out the door, waving at Logan as he approached the car. He flashed a thin smile and hopped in. "I'm sorry I wasn't ready, Mr. and Mrs. Blake," Max said. He didn't mention his missing Bible.

4

COOL SUNDAY SCHOOL

Logan's mom said, "It's okay. The quiet music floated in the air while Logan and Max sat together in the back seat.

"Did you bring your Bible?" Logan asked.

Looking down, Max said, "Nah...I couldn't find it."

"No problem, bro, they've got extra. It'll be fun." Logan said with a smile.

Max smiled, too, feeling better.

They arrived and got out of the car. Passing by the tall fir trees, they walked down the long sidewalk to the propped-open church doors. At the first corridor, Logan and Max turned left to the youth room for fourth through sixth graders. Logan's mom and dad turned right to theirs.

The teacher greeted them. "Hi there, boys! My name is Mr. Keith." He reached to shake Max's hands and asked his name.

"My name is Max."

"Nice to meet you, and welcome to Clark Hill Church!" Mr. Keith said.

"Hey, it's early. Let's hang out. Want to play some foosball?" Logan asked.

Logan introduced Max to his church buddies. "Hey Levi, Ethan, and Eli, this is Max, my friend from school. Oh hey, Isaiah, meet my friend, Max."

Max high-fived the boys and walked to the foosball table. They played, but Max was new at it. He swiveled the rods but missed the kicks, and the ball flew to the side. "Oh man!" said Max, kicking the leg of the table. Logan grinned, but Max turned red.

Mr. Keith called out and waved the kids over to the stage area. The group moseyed over to the rows of chairs and took their seats.

The Sunday School teacher waited, eyes gleaming and relaxed, until everyone was seated.

"Let's pray... Dear Heavenly Father, we come to you today to tell you we love you. We are thankful for what Jesus did for us by dying on the cross. We're so glad He rose from the dead. Lord, we ask the Holy Spirit to move in and through us, in Jesus' name." Mr. Keith said.

Then, a younger blonde man with shoulder-length hair and a white T-shirt and jeans walked up with a guitar, stepped up the platform, and started to play and sing songs about Jesus. He rocked gently back and forth as he played, closing his eyes. Max could see he sang from his heart, and while the worship leader's voice traveled to every ear, Max felt God's love during the worship.

After about fifteen minutes of singing, Mr. Keith got onto the platform and said, "I sense some of you need to make a decision today. I will give some a chance to accept Jesus in their heart."

He usually waited until after telling a Bible story. Still, he felt a sense of urgency, so he prayed,

"Lord, someone here knows they need you right now and knows you are here too, so please touch them and let them know how much you love them." He looked up at the kids and said, "I'm going to lead you in a prayer to help you make Jesus your Savior. It's not the prayer that saves. It's the desire of your heart to make Him Lord that causes Him to respond to you. This prayer only helps you. Class, repeat after me, "Lord, I believe you are the son of God. That you died on the cross for my sins, then rose again from the grave. You did this for me. I ask you to forgive me of all my sins...I now put my faith in you as my Savior; thank you, Jesus. Amen.'"

Tears rolled down Max's face after praying with Mr. Keith because something wonderful had happened. Max now knew Jesus was in his heart and that he was a new person. All his sins were forgiven, like forgetting to take the trash out or disobeying his parents. He felt clean on the inside.

Wiping his eyes, Max sat for the lesson while Logan was beside him, smiling, understanding what had just happened.

Mr. Keith told the story in the Bible of the man of God named Elisha. God told Elisha things to warn and help the King of Israel when an enemy was nearby. One day the King of Aram, Israel's enemy, wanted to find Elisha and capture him because of this. When a report came that Elisha was in Dothan, he sent horses, chariots, and a strong force there. They went by night and surrounded the city.

When Elisha's servant got up early the following

day, an army of horses and chariots surrounded the city.

"Oh no, my Lord! What shall we do?" the servant asked.

"Don't be afraid," Elisha, the prophet, answered. "Those who are with us are more than those who are with them.

And Elisha prayed, "Open his eyes, Lord, so that he may see." Then the Lord opened the servant's eyes, and he looked and saw the hills full of horses and chariots of fire all around Elisha.

God helped Elisha and the king of Israel. Elisha gave God's instructions on what to do, and this band of men went back to their master. So, the bands of Aram stopped raiding Israel's territory."

"You see, kids, like Elisha, God has an army for *you.* Satan, our arch enemy, has his minions too that want to hurt you, but God's army is greater in number and strength!" Mr. Keith said.

"You can always pray for help, and if you need, He can open your eyes to see this spiritual realm too." He continued. "So, remember, kids, when you need help, ask God, and He will help you. Have a good week!" Mr. Keith finished.

After class, he walked up to Max and asked, "Do you have a Bible?"

"I have one at home; I just can't find it."

"That's okay. Please take this one. I've written some things to help you in your new walk with God." Mr. Keith said. "Here, Logan." and handed him a candy bar. Then Mr. Keith said, "See you next week!" All the kids got up and left to find their parents. Logan and Max went down the hallway, met Logan's parents, and walked to the car together.

Sunday School time was great! I want to go again, thought Max. They hopped in the car and drove to Max's house.

"Hey, thanks for the ride!" said Max, and he ran to his home.

From then on, Max went with Logan every week to Sunday School. He was learning a lot and understanding more and more. Realizing how much God always loved and listened to him were favorite things about Him.

5

LIAM'S SECRET

A t school, Max was puzzled about Liam. One day Liam didn't want to play with anyone. He looked sad and kept to himself, only to talk to this toy from his pocket…a little dragon he called his friend.

After school at home, Liam sat alone in his room with a dragon poster hanging above his bed. He lined up the small toys from his favorite adventure video game on his shelf. Locu, Geothorn, and Zapper were his favorites.

His mom worked late, and there was no dad, so he picked up his video game controller and began playing Dragons Of Zotar. He enjoyed the adventure game. Liam read spells on the screen and pushed buttons to activate the spell to win against evil hoards who would block him on his way to the Black Stone. Once at the Black Stone, he re-upped more power and got a spear of fire and shield to go to the next level.

Then, putting the game controller on the floor, he picked up a deck of tarot cards, shuffled them, and laid them face down on the green carpet. Looking at the cards, he picked one up to see it was a red devil with horns and a spiked tail pointing upward. Then a voice whispered, "Give me your life, and I will make you great." Liam thought that sounded good. He liked the idea of being important.

"Okay, devil, I give you my life," whispered Liam. A feeling of power, dark power, filled him.

Falling asleep, Liam dreamed that Locu, a zombie, was chasing him down a dark hallway with a flaming sword. Right before Locu stabbed him, Liam woke up in a sweat.

He laid back down, still shaking from the dream, then picked up his toy dragon, prayed to it, put it on his pillow, and went back to sleep.

In the morning, he tucked his tiny dragon friend

into his pants pocket to bring to school. *It's my only friend,* he thought.

Max, Logan, and Mason saw Liam in class the next day. They walked by him to give him a high five, but Liam only looked down. So, Max gently patted him on the shoulder as they walked by and said, "Hey, friend!"

Liam pounded his fist against his desk. He looked up at Logan with a snarl, wide eyes glowing red. Logan quickly strode over to Mason and Max.

"Did you see that?" whispered Logan. "Liam's eyes turned red!"

"What?" Mason asked quietly. "That's freaky!"

"Yeah, it is," said Logan.

"Must be a reflection," said Max and shrugged it off.

What did that mean? Probably nothing. But it gnawed at Max. *I need to find out more about Liam,* thought Max.

6

THE HOLE

The following day after school, the bell rang, and the kids ran toward the cars waiting for them. They took the school bus some days and got rides in cars other times. Max saw Liam and called out.

"Hey, Liam! Wanna go to the old farm and explore?"

Liam nodded as Max caught up to him.

"Awesome!" said Max. I'll meet you at the folding table

in the field in an hour!"

When Max got dropped off at home, he greeted Echo, checked his dog's food and water, then skipped up the stairs to drop off his backpack and grabbed his cap, and went out the door with Echo.

When Liam and Max met at the card table in the field, they saw where hunters had left the deer head.

"That's so cool!" Max said. Liam nodded. Echo sniffed at the table. "No-no, Echo," Max said.

Liam stared at the deer's head. "I wonder why it's left here?"

"Maybe they forgot it? Max replied.

"Maybe they wanted to give it to the coyotes," Liam said, scratching his head and peering at the brains.

"Yeah, maybe," Max said. "Let's go over there!" pointing to an orchard.

"Sure!" said Liam.

They walked together down a path between orange trees with Echo when Max's sneakers skidded along some loose dirt. He felt himself slipping. The ground gave way! Falling, they slid down into a six-foot hole with the dog! Echo yipped, and the boys yelled! *Thunk!* Max landed on his rear end. Echo fell against him as Liam cartwheeled past, falling into a heap at the bottom of the hole. Dust filled the air and made the boys cough.

"Are you okay, Liam?" Max asked.

"Uh, yeah." *Cough! Cough!* "I think so. What happened?" Liam asked, dusting off his pants. "Some hiding place?"

"I dunno," said Max, looking up to see how far they'd fallen.

Max got up and dusted himself off too. "We're okay."

Echo sneezed. He was okay too, and his tail was wagging to show it. A black dragon toy had slipped out of Liam's pocket.

"Hey, I saw one like this on the other side of the field," Max said.

"Huh," said Liam, picking up his dragon.

"Why do you have that dragon in your pocket?" asked Max.

"He's my friend," said Liam. Then Liam's eyes turned red again. Max stepped back in shock.

"Uh…Uh… what's happening?" said Max.

Liam scrunched his nose, bent down, and picked up a baseball-sized rock. He laughed for no reason, pulling his arm back to throw it at Max.

Max froze, eyes wide, then remembered what Mr. Keith had taught about prayer. He prayed, *Lord, I need you to help Liam. Please stop this.*

As Liam swung his arm and released the rock, it

turned wide and missed Max! Liam fell back and plopped on the dirt, then Liam's eyes became normal.

"What just happened?" asked Liam. He began to tremble, tears rolling down his face.

"I don't know," Max said.

"I don't know what got into me," Liam said, looking down.

"I'm glad you missed me!"

Chuckling, Liam shot a wry smile while wiping his face.

Then Echo barked. Max scanned the opening, searching for a way to crawl out, and prayed silently again,

Lord, we need you. Please help us get out of here. Just then, Max noticed tree roots hanging down from the dirt walls of the hole.

"Look! Let's use the roots to pull ourselves out! But we need to get Echo out first," Max said.

They lifted the dog while grasping the roots for leverage and shoved Echo out. Then Max helped push Liam upward as he gripped the roots. Liam scrambled out. Max pulled himself upward, but his hands began to slip. Max regripped and hoisted himself to the edge, foot slipping, but Liam grabbed his arm and dragged him out. Suddenly…the edge began to crumble!

"Get back!" Max yelled as he pushed Liam away from the collapsing rim.

"Whoa!" cried Liam.

Thump! Liam fell backward from the edge, and Echo jumped back too. Dust rose upward and out all over the boys and the dog.

"Whew!" sighed Max.

"Thanks!" Liam said.

"Hey, thanks to you, I made it out in the first place!" Max said.

Liam's face flushed; he'd never helped anyone like that before. Then all three hurried home as the sun sank low. An angel smiled, hovering over them, watching to see what more he might need to do.

On their way home, Liam saw the dragon toy Max said he'd found. Liam picked it up and handed it to Max.

"Oh, that's the one I was telling you about."

"You can keep it if you like, Max. I have the other one." Liam said.

"Sure, thanks!" Max said. And he placed it in his pocket.

7

TROUBLE TIMES FOUR!

Max, Mason, and Logan ran outside for recess the next day at school. Mason ran for the soccer ball and waved to Max and Logan to play.

Liam came out but stayed back. Max yelled to Liam, "Liam, wanna join?"

"Nah. I don't feel like it today." Liam said as he stepped up on the bench and sat quietly by himself.

He watched the boys play and kick the ball around for a while. Then he heard Max tell Mason and

Logan what happened in the field. He bragged about how Liam helped him out of the hole. Happy to listen to his friends say kind things, he decided to play too. The four ran around kicking the ball to each other until the bell rang for the kids to line up.

Work was being done on the grounds. The boys stood in two lines on the dirt with the rest of the class, waiting for the teacher. It was hot, and they were bored. The teacher took a long time to call them in. Liam decided to pick up a dirt clod. He looked at it, sneered, and threw it at Mason. Mason picked one up and threw it at Liam. Soon, all the kids were throwing dirt clods at each other! It got so loud with screaming and laughter that the poodle-haired teacher ran out. With a red face, she grabbed Max's arm. Then, as she walked up to his friends, she tapped each on the shoulders and said,

"Mason, Logan, and Liam! You four, get to the principal's office right away."

"Oh no! We're in big trouble!" Max cried.

"Why only us four?" Max asked. He thought the principal would make them stand all day, sit in a corner wearing a silly hat, or worse, tell their parents! They shuffled into the office and were directed to sit on a bench next to a big brown door. They waited and waited and waited. Then, the brown door swung open, and Mr. Cromwell, the principal, stood in the tall doorway, nearly hitting his head.

"You four are in trouble," he scowled, hands on his hips. "Come in and sit here."

Mason, Max, Logan, and Liam went in and sat in the four chairs. Mr. Cromwell parked behind his huge oak desk, peering at Liam over his glasses.

Left hand rubbing his bald head, he said, "Boys, you should *not* have thrown those dirt clods! You could have hurt someone. If I ever catch you again, your parents will be told, and you will be removed from school, never to come back again!"

Max sat stone-still with the others. He felt bad for going along with the dirt clod fight. He told the principal he was sorry and would never do that again. The other three nodded in agreement.

The principal waved his hand and said, "Go back to class."

"Whew!" said Max turning to Mason. "That won't happen again!"

Mason agreed, as did Logan. Liam scrunched his nose.

All four shuffled along down the hall toward their classroom, somber, not talking to each other for the rest of the day. Max felt close with each friend, though, like they were *partners in crime*, including Liam.

They walked into class and sat at their desks.

Max was relieved to be out of the principal's office.

8

FOUND IT!

Max left school that day. When he got home, he took his schoolbooks and went downstairs to do homework but decided to look for his Bible instead. Echo trailed behind; Max turned over pillows and books and opened drawers. Still nothing.

He hadn't taken out the trash, so he got up to begin collecting, glad to have a break from thinking too much. Dragging the large trash bag, he went into each room to gather, determined to finish his schoolwork before Mom came home. Mom and Dad's room- done, Marian's- done, and now Mile's room. In Mile's bedroom, he picked up the waste can when he spied a familiar book pushed behind some of the toys. *Was that his missing Bible?*

He walked over to it, moved the toys away, and sure enough, it **was** the missing Bible! *But why would Miles hide my Bible?* Max thought. He took his Bible and went to his room. He also wondered what to say to Miles when he got home. Grabbing his homework, he strode down the stairs and plopped on the couch.

Later, Miles, Marian, Mom, and Dad came through the door. Mom was happy to see Max doing his homework!

"How was your day?" his mom asked.

Looking up, Max said, "Good…well, I kinda got into trouble." Max said.

"What happened?" Mom asked as she sat

opposite him on the coffee table.

"We were caught throwing dirt clods," said Max, looking down.

"Oh, Max! Then what happened?"

A teacher made us go to the principal's office, yelling at us never to do that again. Mom, I was so scared." Max said.

"Oh, dear…Anything else?" Mom inquired.

"He said if we were caught doing that again, we would never be able to come back to school, *sniff*," Max said.

"Oh, Maximus. You knew better than that." Mom said.

"I know, but it all just went crazy. Liam started it, then we were just all doing it," said Max shrugging.

"But Maximus, you knew better." pleaded Mom.

"I know, I know. I'm sorry, Mom. I won't do that again and told the principal that too."

"I'm sure you won't," said Mom patting Max's hand on his knee. "I think you've had your punishment already," and leaned over and hugged Max, her red hair spilling onto his wet face.

"Sniff. Thanks, Mom."

She smiled and went to the kitchen.

While Dad, Miles, and Marian had been snacking in the dining room, Max sat there, taking a deep breath.

He heard footsteps, looked up, and saw them walk upstairs to their bedrooms.

Max slipped from the couch and quietly followed Miles upstairs to his bedroom. He prayed under his breath, not knowing how Miles would react to him about his Bible.

"What's up?" asked Miles.

"While collecting the trash in your room, I found my Bible hidden behind your toys," said Max. "Why was it hidden in your room?

"I...um... don't know," said Miles, shrugging.

"I don't get it, Miles. You act like it's fun to make me mad!" Max said.

"Well, it is!" Miles snapped. Surprised, Max prayed in his mind asking the Lord for help. Then, Miles felt guilt *and* love come over him like God touched his heart.

"But... I'm sorry." Miles said. "Since you came along, Dad and Mom have given you more attention than me. I am sorry."

"I forgive you, Miles," Max said. Mile's eyes slackened as he nudged the carpet with his sneaker. He'd never felt guilt *plus* love before.

Max turned and walked to his room with Echo.

9

The Closet

The room was quiet. Echo jumped up onto Max's bed and flopped in a heap! Max sat next to his dog, patting his happy head! He was also happy-- that he had his Bible back but grateful for the one Mr. Keith gave him. In fact, the one Mr. Keith had given him made him curious about how different it might be, so he opened it to a blank page and read what the teacher wrote.

"But you will receive power when the Holy Spirit has come upon you, and you will be my witnesses in Jerusalem and in all Judea and Samaria, and to the end of the earth." Acts 1:8

"For this reason, I tell you, whatever you ask in prayer, believe that you have received it, and it will be yours." Mark 11:24

"For I know the plans I have for you, declares the LORD, plans for welfare and not for evil, to give you a future and a hope. Then you will call upon me and come and pray to me, and I will hear you. You will seek me and find me when you seek me with all your heart." Jeremiah 29:11-13

But you, when you pray, enter into your closet and lock your door, and pray to your Father who is in secret, and your Father who sees in secret will reward you in public. Matthew 6:6

"Wooooaaa." Max enjoyed reading these verses Mr. Keith wrote. He walked into his closet, closed the door, climbed over his shoes, and sat. He couldn't lock it, but it was shut, at least. Echo sat outside of the closet whimpering quietly.

"Shhhhhh, Echo. It's okay. I'll be out soon," said Max behind the closet door.

He bowed his head in the dark and started talking to Jesus.

"Lord, you know I'm really new at this. It's been a hard day. Please forgive me for throwing dirt clods at the other kids. But thank you for helping me with Miles. I'm happy Miles apologized. It's been tough hanging out with Liam, though. There is something kinda dark about him…he needs you, Lord. And I need you. Thanks for protecting me from the rock Liam threw, for what I don't know. But I know you're with me. Thanks for helping me with Miles. Thanks for giving me Logan as a friend. Please help me help my friends know you, too. I ask you to fill me with the Holy Spirit so I can have your power to be good and to tell my friends about you."

Echo scratched at the closet door. "Okay, okay, Echo. I'm coming out." Max felt peace and joy, as if God was hugging him. It was amazing.

He opened the closet door. Echo's tail went in circles seeing his buddy.

"Time for dinner!" his mom yelled.

Max spun out of his room and raced down the stairs to the dining room, Echo at his heels.

The family was waiting and looked at Max in wonder. There was something about him. His face was gleaming, and he smiled as wide as a watermelon.

"Sweetheart, there is something about you! Mom

said, looking at Max.

"Mom, I just spent time with the Lord and feel so happy," Max replied.

His mom lowered her head and didn't say anything. Miles, Marian, and Dad were quiet as if pondering what that meant. And something stopped any criticism, like the Bible story when an angel of the Lord protected Daniel by closing the mouths of the lions.

The family finished their dinner and went their separate ways. The kids went upstairs to finish their homework while Dad and Mom watched TV in the living room.

Max flopped onto his bed with Echo next to him. Echo licked Max's arm over and over again, but Max didn't care this time. He thought about how God had touched his heart and heard everything he said.

10

GET TOGETHER

Max, Logan, and Mason ran outside for recess after hours of writing and math. They couldn't wait to see the blue sky and feel the fresh air on their faces. "Your it!" said Logan as he ran from Max.

Max dashed for the nearest boy--it was Liam. Liam was standing alone under a tree, but when Max tagged him, Liam decided to play too. Liam raced for Mason, who was trying not to get tagged but tripped over a ridge on the ground. Liam caught him.

"Tag! Your it now!" said Liam.

The boys laughed as they kept tagging each other until it was time for class. They stopped at the drinking fountain before lining up.

"Hey guys!" said Max. Let's go to Liam's house after school! The guys liked the idea, but Liam wasn't sure.

"No one's home when I get there. Mom says I'm not supposed to have friends when she's not home."

"Oh, man!" Max said. "What about when she does get home?"

"I'll have to ask," said Liam.

"Yeah, let us know, okay?" Max said.

"Okay," Liam said.

"Hey, I have an idea; why don't you guys come to my house after school tomorrow," asked Logan. "Then you can all go with me to the youth group?"

"What's youth group?" asked Liam.

"It's kids getting together to have fun, sing, and play games and stuff," said Logan. "I'll check with my mom and let you know."

"Cool!" all the boys said together.

The school bell rang, letting all the kids know to head to class. Max walked fast, but Logan had just texted his mom and caught up to him.

"Max! Mom said all the guys can come over after school, and then she'll bring us all to youth group in the evening!" Logan said.

Mason and Liam caught up to them after lagging behind and heard the word too. "Great!" said Mason. Liam looked down and wasn't sure he really wanted to go.

"I don't know," Liam said.

"It's so much fun!" said Logan. "Besides, we get to hear really cool music and a great message from our Sunday School teacher, Mr. Keith.

"Umm...I don't know." Liam said, scrunching his nose again.

"We really want you to come with us, Liam!" Mason said.

Liam scratched his head and walked on to class. He'd never had such friends before. Mason, Logan, and Max paced to make sure they got to class on time.

The next day during recess, the boys gathered to talk. Liam dragged his feet as he got close to his friends. He fidgeted too, which was new. Max, Logan, and Mason clapped as Liam joined them. Liam looked up at each face and knew he was a friend too.

Logan asked Liam, "So, are you in?"

"Yeah..." Liam said.

"Hooray!!" all the boys cried.

Max noticed Liam was happier. But he didn't understand why Liam didn't want to go to church for youth group.

"Let's play!" cried Max.

So off they went, kicking the soccer ball around, making sure Liam could keep up.

11

POOL

P iling out of Logan's mom's car, they stumbled and laughed at Mason's silly joke.

"That joke was terrible!" laughed Logan.

"Hey, my dad told me that joke yesterday, and I thought it was funny," said Mason.

"But it's a *dad* joke!" Max said, laughing. Those are never funny!

They walked down the long sidewalk, with the fir

trees blocking the setting sun. The church doors were open, and they could hear music. Liam plodded beside them, hands shaking.

As the four strode along the hallway, Mr. Keith stood at the youth room door, bobbing to the music with his curly black hair and waving the kids into the room. *The music was so cool!* mused Max.

Kids in the room were playing pool or ping pong at the tables. Girls from school, Jordan and Hailey, recognized the boys and waved with smiles. Max eyed the snacks! Mrs. Keith, Logan called her, was serving lemonade and cookies. One of the girls, Naomi, came over with a cup of lemonade to offer to Liam. She was a greeter and helped new kids feel welcome. Isaiah, Logan's friend, came over to them. His blue T-shirt read in bold letters, "HIS," with a scripture under the letters.

"Hey, guys! What's up?" Isaiah said. Liam fidgeted. When Isaiah held out his hand to shake Liam's, Liam stretched out his to shake hands too. Isaiah smiled so big that Liam couldn't help but smile back.

Logan put his arm around his buddy Isaiah's shoulder as they walked to a pool table. Isaiah picked up a cue stick and said, "Hey Logan, let's play in teams! You and I are a team, and Max and Liam are a team. Then Mason is next."

Max also picked up a cue stick and remembered

playing with his uncle. Liam slowly picked up a cue stick but stood still, staring at the pool table, not knowing what to do.

Isaiah stepped over and explained to Liam how to play the game. Max nodded in agreement.

They played until they heard the music.

Some adult and teen helpers were gathered in a corner, holding hands in prayer together.

12

CLOSE ENCOUNTERS
OF A DRAGON KIND

L ogan asked, "Did you feel that?".
"Feel what?" Max responded.
"Something's wrong, but I'm not sure
what it is."

Max glanced over at Liam, motioned, and said,
"Logan, look at Liam."
"Yeah, he's *really* fidgety. We need to pray," said

Logan.

The two of them slipped off to pray.

"Lord, help Liam," Logan prayed, remembering the Bible story. "I bet there're angels in here,"

Max nodded.

Angels filled the room, wings spread.

A helper waved and called the kids to sit near the stage. Logan, Max, Mason, and Liam sat together in the third row. Liam got very wiggly again, and his hands were still shaking. Max noticed it and asked if he was okay. Liam only nodded.

Mr. Keith stepped up to the stage and said a prayer for the meeting, then stepped down so everyone could see the words on the screen and sing along. They called it worship. Liam shifted in his seat a lot. A few hands went into the air, and Max looked down, praying. In his mind's eye, he could see angels in the room.

A dark figure floated in and lingered at the door. The angels above quickly leaned forward in battle position, hands on their swords, ready to draw them. As soon as the dark reptile slithered further, swords were out. Suddenly, the dark figure swirled into a 20-foot-tall dragon! Its eyes glowed red, glaring at the angels while it neared Liam. Max felt cold, and his hair stood on the back of his neck. He reached and propped up his collar to get warmer. The dragon, covered in slimy black scales, eyed Liam with a sneer and hovered over Liam during the worship.

The musicians stopped. Mr. Keith took the stage and began to pray. He felt, once again, the need to ask if anyone wanted to accept Jesus as their Savior. If so, they could walk up to the stage to be prayed with. Max looked at Liam and Liam at Max. Liam continued to wriggle.

Max whispered to Liam, "Do you want me to go up there with you?"

Liam trembled. "Ya...ya...yes." I...I... I do! But I'm scared...really scared right now." Max pulled on Liam's arm, and the dragon lunged with a hiss. A black cloud engulfed Liam, and he slumped in his seat.

Mr. Keith prayed. "Father, in the name of Jesus, we ask you to free those bound by the devil. Release them so they can come to you."

At that, the angels closed in toward the dragon, swords blazing. The dragon lashed out with its claws, but a hot blade sliced the claw, and it fell to the floor. The black reptile screamed and swung its tail at an angel. That angel blocked the tail hard with its luminous wings. The dragon recoiled. Another mighty angel flew above the dragon's head, swinging his arcing sword in circles to strike. The dragon grabbed Liam's throat, and Liam began coughing. The angel above swung down and grabbed his claw and pulled it off Liam's throat. Liam fell to the floor, gasping.

Mr. Keith ran over with helpers to Liam. They gently laid their hands on Liam and began to pray.

"Lord, we ask you to bind any demon latching on to Liam." Mr. Keith said.

More angels joined the fight. They wrapped the dragon with bands and tied him up. Strapped his snout, bound its claws to his tail folding the dragon in half, and dragged him out of the room, **Whoosh! ...** leaving a wake of red smoke.

The room grew quiet. The unseen realm became calm. The remaining angels floated backward to the ceiling, wings spread to hover, guarding against further attack. Liam relaxed. Opening his eyes to see the smiling faces surrounding him, Mr. Keith asked if Liam would pray with him, and he smiled and nodded. He prayed with the Sunday School teacher to invite Jesus into his heart.

"Liam, pray this prayer after me..." Mr. Keith said. Liam nodded.

"Dear Jesus..." Mr. Keith said.

"Dear Jesus..." Liam repeated.

"I believe you are the Son of God...."

"I believe you are the Son of God...."

"I believe you died for my sins and rose again...."

"I believe you died for my sins and rose again...."

"And I invite you into my heart to be my Savior."

"I invite you into my heart to be my Savior...

"Amen."

"Amen."

Now, Liam felt peace. Max, Logan, and Mason could see a new joy on Liam's face. Mason had not yet prayed and asked Mr. Keith if he could also ask Jesus into his heart. Mr. Keith was happy to do so and prayed with Mason. It was time for the message; Liam and Mason were ready to hear the Word and grow in the Lord.

Meanwhile, angels were having a party and praising the Savior who gave eternal life to two more souls and made them win the battle over the dragon. Throwing glow balls and glitter, they also played sword fighting in celebration, and as Mr. Keith taught, the room became lighter and brighter.

Mr. Keith explained how new believers should burn anything having to do with witchcraft, tarot cards, anything representing Satan, devil-like pictures, games, and toys. Liam sat and absorbed it all while Max rested and listened.

Mr. Keith spent extra time talking to Liam before the night was over. Logan's parents walked into the youth room, so the four boys ran to meet them and told them all that had happened.

13

LIAM'S LAST STAND

The boys were home all snug in their beds, thinking about that night. Each had an angel in their room, hovering above, keeping watch. But Liam sensed something evil in the room too. Then he remembered what Mr. Keith taught.

"Mom!" called Liam.

"Yes, Liam," his mom said. It was late, but she was home from work.

"Mom, I want to get rid of some of my toys."

"Why, honey, it's late. Let's talk about it in the morning, okay?" Mom said.

"Okay." Liam rolled over and tried to go to sleep.

But the hair on his neck stood up, and a pair of red eyes leered at Liam from the corner of his room in the unseen realm. He felt it.

"Lord, help me!" he whispered. Then the Holy Spirit spoke through Liam and gave him a voice not his own.

"You must leave in the name of Jesus!" Liam cried out. *Swoosh!* The evil presence fled. Liam turned over and went fast to sleep.

The following day was Saturday, and his mom was home. Liam reminded his mom that he wanted to get rid of some toys and things. His mom was pleased because she didn't like some of Liam's stuff.

"Mom, will you let me burn them?"

"What on earth for?" his mom said.

"I would just feel better, Mom," Liam said.

"All right. Get your things, Liam, and put them all in this bag, then we'll toss them into the BBQ," she said. Liam was relieved his mom was okay with doing that.

He quickly went through his demonic toys and things and placed them all in the bag his mom gave him.

His Zotar dragon poster, characters from his video game like Locu, Geothorn, and Zapper, his video game Dragon of Zotar, his dragon toy he prayed to, tarot cards, an Ouija board, and a horoscope game. "Here, Mom!" Liam said as he handed the bag to her.

She took it outside to the BBQ, placed the bag inside, poured lighter fluid on the bag, struck a match, and both watched it all burn. When she did, Liam felt a new delight deep in his heart! He couldn't wait to go back to the youth group with Max, Logan, and Mason and tell them what he did!

14

THE DRAGON SLAYER

Max stumbled over his Siberian husky, getting out of bed. The dog jumped, wagging his fluffy tail. It was Saturday and a day free from school! Max ran out the back door to enjoy the outside with Echo hightailing behind.

The sky was bluer, and the grass was greener. Max felt light inside and joy like never before. With Mr.

Keith's Bible in hand, he planted himself under their oak tree as the breeze blew his dark brown hair away from his eyes. It felt good. He turned to the place Mr. Keith had marked and reread the verses. Ruffled by the wind, Max kept his hand on the white pages.

Crack! The fence split! His white dog beside him jumped to his feet and started barking, the back of his neck hair standing up! Max looked up to see the neighbor's black Doberman smash through the rotting fence, standing four feet from them, growling. Above, a large crimson dragon drifted over the dog nearing Max. His bat-like wings stretched wide to cover his prey, claws flexing for an attack, and Max sensed the evil presence near him.

The dragon snorted, red eyes sharpened against Max, whipping his tail around. The Doberman grew angrier as the tip of the dragon's tail snapped at the dog. The Doberman stepped slowly toward Max, baring his teeth.

Max cried out, "Lord, I don't know what to do. Help me!" As if in a dream, Max lifted his Bible and said, "Get away in the name of Jesus! The Lord rebuke you!"

A fiery angel swooped down like lightning on the dragon and stabbed its chest. The dragon screamed, spreading red smoke all over the yard, then vanished in a red puff! The angel smiled in victory, gliding upward with shimmering wings spread and piercing blue eyes shining like the sun.

The Doberman pivoted and ran through the break in the fence. Max couldn't believe what had come out of his mouth! He got up and ran to tell his mom, with Echo close behind. As he ran, he stepped and broke a toy hidden by the tall grass. Max picked up the broken toy and recognized it right away. He had broken the dragon Liam gave him, dropped it earlier in the week, and carried it to his mom.

He told his mom what happened, and she hugged Max, relieved he was okay.

"Oh, Max! You could have been hurt very badly!"

"Mom, I know God was with me and protected me," Max said.

"You know, Max, ever since you've accepted Jesus, I've seen you face and overcome very difficult things," his mom said. "You've become very brave, and I think God *is* really with you! I don't understand it all, but I think I'd like to give you a nickname. *Max, The Dragon Slayer!*

***

"For we are not fighting against flesh and blood enemies, but against evil rulers and authorities of the unseen world, against mighty powers in this dark world, and against evil spirits in the heavenly places." Ephesians 6:12

***

Jesus said to them, "Behold, I was watching Satan fall from heaven like lightning.
Behold, I have given you authority to tread on serpents and scorpions and over all the power of the enemy, and nothing will injure you.
Nevertheless, do not rejoice at this, that the spirits are subject to you, but rejoice that your names are recorded in heaven." Luke 10:18-20

~The End~

Special Points from the Author:

- This story is fiction, but the reality of a spiritual world where angels and demons exist is true.
- Where eyes turn red, have been discerned by Christians in demonized people.
- It is true that when people play demonic games, try witchcraft with spells, or use tarot cards or spell books, they open themselves up to demons.
- The simple prayer for salvation, unless sincere, does not save you. As you pray, you must put true faith and trust in the Lord Jesus Christ.
- Anyone can be free of demonization if they want to be. Fasting with prayer breaks the stronghold in the surrendered-to-Christ person.
- Also, the book of Acts shows an example of getting rid of occult material like Liam does in the story. It is important to rid oneself of such things as it destroys the entry points.

> "And many of those who practiced magical arts collected their books and [throwing book after book on a pile] began burning them in front of everyone. They calculated their value and found it to be 50,000 pieces of silver."
> Acts 19:19

"In US dollars, that would be about 5.5 million today!" ~David Guzik

If you prayed the prayer of salvation with Liam or Max and were sincere, then Jesus came into your heart and gave you eternal life! I'm so happy for you! And Jesus said, "I tell you, there is rejoicing in the presence of the angels of God over one sinner who repents." Luke 15:10

- Now it's time to grow in the Lord.
- Attend a local Bible-believing church.
- Get a Bible and read it daily.
- Pray and worship Him often.
- If you ask the Holy Spirit to baptize you, he will give you the power to share your faith with others!

Now, go and share what God has done for you. Maybe even give this book to someone you know who needs it. May the Lord protect and bless you, dear reader.

About the Author

Merry is a children's book writer and illustrator now but spent years telling stories with principles to children from around the world. Her passion began at age fourteen, recounting famous sagas in the classroom by age nineteen. She was awarded second place as Best Teacher at then mega-church Melodyland Christian Center in 1976.

Illustrating and writing devotions for her sister-in-law inspired a desire to publish. Eventually, she published her first work, a poem in an anthology. A course from the Institute Of Children's Literature fueled her eagerness to write for kids, but she later published blogs targeting Christian audiences. Finally, in 2016, her dream came true with the publication of her first picture book, *Lolly's Fish Tale; When She Meets A Bully Face To Face*, where she wrote and illustrated the book with her daughter, Kelly Galusha, as her digital painter bringing Merry's illustrations to life. Since then, she has continued to work on children's books, keeping her growing grandchildren in mind.

When she's not preparing for her various callings, Merry loves hiking with her husband, Rick, where they live in Southern California, or visiting their kids and grandchildren in Tennessee.

https://www.facebook.com/Merry.S.Streeter

Acknowledgments

I want to thank my husband, who always supports me during the writing, editing, and publication process. He is my rock beside my Rock. A thank you to my family, who patiently waited for this book to come out.

A thank you to Debby Johnson, who edited the manuscript thoroughly and whose advice I mostly applied. Also, Dennis Knotts, who also edited the story and helped polish the rough spots too.

Thank you to dear friends in The Book Binder Writers' Group and from my Facebook Author Page, those who cheered me on and gave their input.

Thank you to all other friends who knew this book was coming out and encouraged with their love and support!

Don't miss her first children's book:
Lolly's Fish Tale;
When She Meets A Bully Face To Face
You can buy it on Amazon.com,
Barnes&Noble.com, and Authorhouse.com

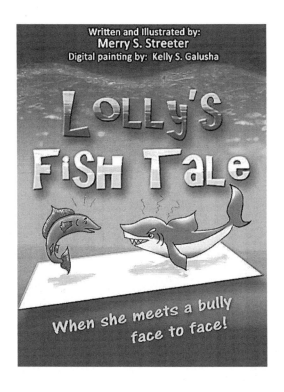

Get her second book, a short story called,
Apollumi; Journey To The Great King
on Amazon.com!

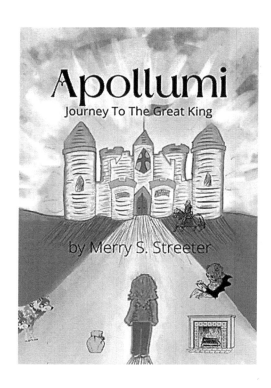